This book belongs to

....

This is the story of Coralie,

a mermaid princess, living under the sea.

There's something else in this story as well.

On every page, can you find the seashell?

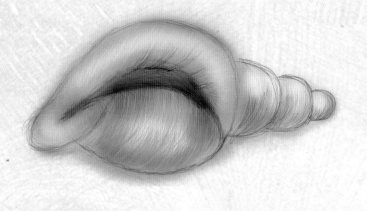

This edition first published in 2010 by Castle Street Press
an imprint of make believe ideas ltd.

Copyright © 2007 make believe ideas ltd
27 Castle Street, Berkhamsted, Hertfordshire, HP4 2DW, UK.
565, Royal Parkway, Nashville, TN 37214, USA.

Little Mermaid

Illustrations by
Katie Saunders

A mermaid princess
lives under the sea.
Her name is Coralie.

One day, Prince Peter
falls out of his boat.
He cannot swim.
Coralie saves him.

"I love Prince Peter!"
says Coralie.
"I want to be a girl!"

11

Coralie goes to see Seaweedy Nora.

"I want to be a girl!"
says Coralie.

Seaweedy
Nora

"Drink this and you
will be a girl,"
says Seaweedy Nora.
"But first you must
put your voice into this shell."

Now Coralie has legs.
She can walk.
But she cannot talk.

Coralie sees Prince Peter
in his boat.

Prince Peter sees Coralie.
He kisses her.
Seaweedy Nora is angry!

Seaweedy Nora takes the shell
and uses Coralie's voice.
She calls the prince and he
comes to her.
Coralie cannot speak.

The birds fly to
Seaweedy Nora.
They break the shell.

Prince Peter and Coralie
are very happy together.

Ready to tell

Oh no! Some of the pictures from this story have been mixed up! Can you retell the story and point to each picture in the correct order?

Picture dictionary

Encourage your child to read these words from the story and gradually develop his or her basic vocabulary.

birds

boat

girl

legs

mermaids

prince

sea

shell

swim

I • up • look • we • like • and • on • at • for •

Key words

Here are some key words used in context. Help your child to use other words from the border in simple sentences.

Coralie **is** a mermaid.

She saves Prince Peter.

Coralie **goes** to see Seaweedy Nora.

Coralie **sees** the boat.

The prince and Coralie **are** very happy.

Left border (top to bottom): am • can • yes • it • see • she • me • of • was • went • in • come • get • day

Right border (top to bottom): a • he • is • said • go • you • are • this • going • they • away • play • cat • to

• the • dog • big • my • mom • no • dad • all •

Make a starfish necklace

Would you like to be a mermaid? Why not put on a bikini top, wrap your legs in shiny material, and make this beautiful starfish necklace?

You will need

white glue • a toothpick • waxed paper • sand or glitter • a paper clip • narrow ribbon or cord

What to do

1 Carefully squeeze some glue onto the waxed paper, in the shape of a small starfish. Use the toothpick to help shape the glue.

2 Ask an adult to bend a paper clip into a "V" shape.

3 Put the ends of a paper clip into the glue at the end of one arm of the starfish.

4 Sprinkle the glue lightly with sand or glitter.

5 Gently shake off the excess sand or glitter.

6 Let it dry completely. (This will take all night and sometimes longer.)

7 Carefully peel the waxed paper off the back of the starfish.

8 Thread about $1\frac{1}{2}$ feet ($\frac{1}{2}$ meter) of narrow ribbon, or other cord, through the paper clip. Tie it in a knot.

Slip the necklace over your head and sing like a mermaid!